★ American Girl™

Emerson Is
Mighty
Girl!

Adapted by Meredith Rusu
from the screenplay by Kati Rocky

Scholastic Inc.

americangirl.com/service

ISBN 978-1-338-25431-0

10 9 8 7 6 5 4 3 2 1   18 19 20 21 22

Printed in the U.S.A.   40
First printing 2018

Book design by Carolyn Bull

Animation art direction by
Jessica Rogers and Riley Wilkinson

Scholastic Inc.
557 Broadway, New York, NY 10012

It's a beautiful day in the garden.
The WellieWishers are playing
Garden Superheroes.

Ashlyn is Glitter Girl.
She has a super sparkle wand.
Camille is Agent Eagle Eyes.
She has super vision.

And Willa is Captain Quick.
She has super speed.
They are all looking for the
Wicked Wellie of the West.
Where, oh where, can she be?

There she is!

Kendall is pretending to be the Wicked Wellie of the West.

"You can't stop me from destroying your precious garden," she says.

Just then, Emerson leaps down
from a tree.

"The Wicked Wellie of the West
is no match for me," she says.
"I am . . . Mighty Girl!"

"You're not getting your hands on our garden," cries Emerson. She charges ahead and catches the Wicked Wellie of the West!

The other girls catch up.

"Why did you run ahead like that?" Willa asks.

"We're supposed to defeat the Wicked Wellie of the West together," Camille says.

"I'm so mighty, I can catch her all by myself!" says Emerson.

"That's no fun," says Willa. "I call a do-over."

The friends play again.

But this time, Emerson pretends to have all the superpowers.

"We're not going to play if Mighty Girl keeps hogging all the superpowers," says Ashlyn.

"We might as well go get our picnic stuff."

"Should I make a mighty dash for it?" asks Emerson.

"No!" shout the WellieWishers.

The WellieWishers head to their garden playhouse.

They put sandwiches, lemonade, and a watermelon for their picnic into the carriage.

They bring a soccer ball and a kite to play with, too.

"It's picnic time," Ashlyn
says. "Let's go!"

But Emerson is still feeling
mighty. She pushes the carriage
too fast and hits a rock.

CRASH!

Food spills everywhere!

Now her friends are upset.
"Please give it a rest with
Mighty Girl," says Ashlyn.
"Mighty Girl is mighty tiring,"
says Kendall. "Just be the real
Emerson for now."

Emerson still wants to be
Mighty Girl.
But she agrees to try being
herself for a little while.

At the picnic, all the girls are having fun . . . except Emerson.

She wishes she could still pretend to be Mighty Girl. It made her feel special.

Emerson wants to prove that she really is Mighty Girl. She has an idea.

"Hey guys, check out Mighty Girl's supersonic strength!" she says. She picks up the watermelon.

Emerson tries to lift the
watermelon, but it's too heavy.
She drops it!

SPLAT!

Sticky pieces of watermelon
fly everywhere.

The watermelon was holding down the kite.

Now a gust of wind picks up the kite. It floats away into a tall tree.

The other WellieWishers are covered in watermelon.

And now their kite is stuck.

"That's enough!" they cry.

"We don't want Mighty Girl at the picnic anymore," says Willa.

"We like Emerson, not Mighty Girl," Camille adds.

But Emerson does not listen.
She pushes the carriage up the
hill toward the tree.

"Never fear," she says.
"Mighty Girl will fix this using
her colossal climbing powers!
I will climb the carriage and
grab the kite and then—"

Oh no!
The carriage rolls back down
the hill and right through
the picnic.
CRASH!

Emerson's friends run over.
"Are you okay?" they ask.
"Yes," Emerson says sadly. She
looks at the mess. "But the picnic
isn't.
"The only superpowers I have
are making my friends mad.
I'm sorry."

"We're not mad at you," says Willa. "We just like the real Emerson better than Mighty Girl."

"You do?" asks Emerson.

"Of course!" say her friends.

That gives Emerson an idea.
"Mighty Girl may have ruined
the day. But I know who can save it."

The other WellieWishers groan. "Oh no. Mighty Girl again?" "Nope." Emerson smiles. "Me! I will use my super cleaning powers to get rid of this super mess."

Emerson works quickly to clean up the mess she made.

"Wow. You are mighty good at cleaning up!" her friends say. "That was amazing."

"You see," says Ashlyn. "The real Emerson is the best of all."

Emerson grins.

She may not be a real superhero, but as long as the WellieWishers are her friends, she feels very super indeed!

Turn the page
for a paper doll of
Emerson!

Emerson

To dress your Emerson paper doll:

1. Ask an adult to help you carefully cut out the clothing and accessories. Be sure to cut along all solid black lines, including slots.

2. Fold the tabs on the dotted lines and attach clothing and accessories to your paper doll. Some tabs have slots to connect them together to help the clothes stay on better.

3. To attach Emerson's cape, simply wrap it around her neck.

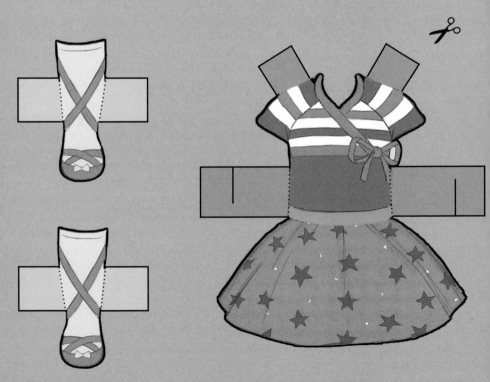

The tabs on Emerson's play pieces can be folded back along the dotted lines to allow the items to stand up.

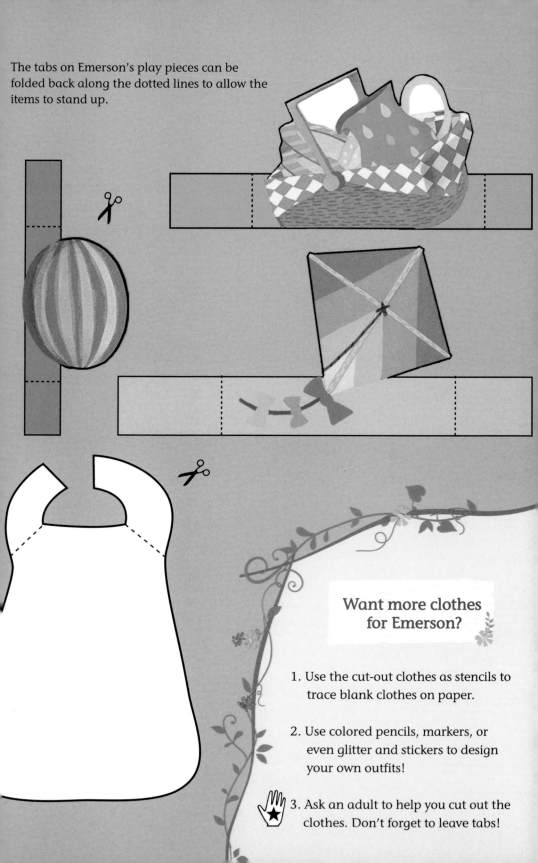

Want more clothes for Emerson?

1. Use the cut-out clothes as stencils to trace blank clothes on paper.

2. Use colored pencils, markers, or even glitter and stickers to design your own outfits!

3. Ask an adult to help you cut out the clothes. Don't forget to leave tabs!

To put together your paper doll and stand:

1. Carefully press out the Emerson figure.

2. Press out the two rectangular pieces. These will be the stand for the doll.

3. Find the slots labeled C on the stand pieces and fit them together.

4. Fit slots A and B on the stand pieces into slots A and B under Emerson's feet.

5. Now you are ready to dress and accessorize Emerson!

6. The tabs on Carrot the bunny can be folded back along the dotted lines to allow Carrot to stand up.

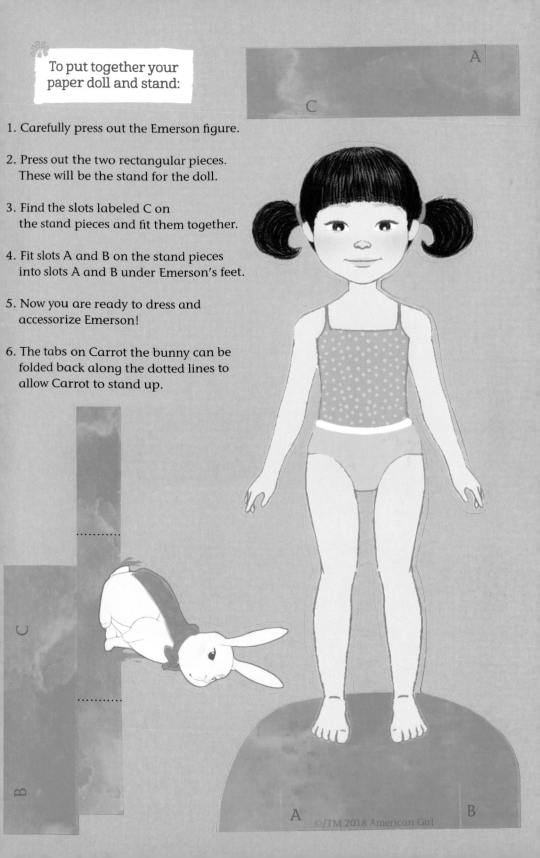

A

C

C

B

A

B

©/TM 2018 American Girl

Meredith Rusu

Emerson is
Mighty Girl

DATE	ISSUED TO